A MAGIC CIRCLE BOOK

BOY IN THE MIDDLE

written by **GLADYS BAKER BOND** illustrated by **TRINA HYMAN**

THEODORE CLYMER
SENIOR AUTHOR, READING 360

GINN AND COMPANY
A XEROX COMPANY

There were three Dugan boys—
Tim, Mick, and Pat. Mick was
the one in the middle.

Mick and his brothers had fun.
They liked to do the same things.
They went to the same school.
They had the same friends. The
Dugan brothers got along well.

But Mick had a problem. For
as long as he could remember,
people had said, "You're one of
the Dugan boys. But which one
are you?"

The Dugan boys looked alike. They all had blue eyes, red hair, and freckles. They were all about the same size. Pat was big for his age. Tim was short. Mick was just right.

The boys talked alike too. Sometimes Grandmother said, "Look at me when you talk. I like to see who I'm talking to."

Looking alike and talking alike were fine with Tim and Pat.

"I don't see why this is a problem for you," Dad said to Mick. "Mother and I treat you all alike."

Mick thought about what Dad had said. But he was not Tim Dugan. And he was not Pat Dugan. He was Mick Dugan and that's the way he wanted people to think of him.

7

One night at dinner Mick
said, "I want to be thought of as
ME."

"What do you mean?" asked
Grandmother. "What can you do?"

"I don't know," Mick answered.

"I can make faces," Pat said.

"You're the funny one around here," said Dad.

"And I can run fast and play ball and swim too," Tim added.

9

But Mick was not funny. And he was not good at games. He was just one of the Dugan boys.

"Maybe you could find something you like to do," Grandmother said. But Mick just shook his head.

"May I please go now?" he asked his dad. "I told Mrs. Smith I would walk her dog." So Mick went to Mrs. Smith's.

And the following day Mick played with the James children while Mrs. James went to the store. Then Mick helped Mr. Pate find his glasses. And he took the cans out to the street for Mrs. Mead.

People did not pay Mick for all the things he did for them. People needed help, so Mick helped them.

That week some people named Cook moved into the building. One day Mick met Mrs. Cook in the elevator. Mick guessed what Mrs. Cook was going to say. And she said it.

"You're one of the Dugan boys. But which one are you?"

Mrs. Smith, Mrs. James, Mrs. Mead, and Mr. Pate were in the elevator too. Mrs. Smith said, "This is Mick Dugan. He's the friendly Dugan boy."

Mick smiled. He had his answer.
He was the FRIENDLY Dugan
boy!

When Mick walked out of the building, he met one of his mother's friends. "You're one of the Dugan boys," she said. "But which one are you?"

"I'm the friendly Dugan boy," he answered. And he smiled. Being in the middle wasn't as bad as he had thought!

ABCDEFGHIJK 7654321
PRINTED IN THE UNITED STATES OF AMERICA